CAPTAIN VALIANT

THE MAN WHO STOLE A PLANET

ADAM BRITTEN

Illustrated by Arthur Hamer

Piccadilly

For Lynn

First published in Great Britain in 2013
by Piccadilly Press Ltd,
A Templar/Bonnier publishing company
Deepdene Lodge, Deepdene Avenue,
Dorking, Surrey, RH5 4AT
www.piccadillypress.co.uk

A catalogue record for this book is available
from the British Library

ISBN: 978 1 84812 347 2 (paperback)

1 3 5 7 9 10 8 6 4 2

Printed and bound by
CPI Group (UK) Ltd, Croydon, CR0 4YY
Cover design by Simon Davis
Cover and interior illustrations by Arthur Hamer

SOME STUFF YOU MIGHT NEED TO KNOW

OK, before we get started, let's talk about me. After all, I'm the one telling the story.

My name is Mark Taylor and I'm an Astral Guardian. So are my dad, mum and sister. We've been sent to Earth to protect the world from super villains, aliens and all sorts of nasty stuff. We're part of an intergalactic police force whose job it is to make sure the universe stays safe. Astral Command (who are in charge of just about everything) give us our orders but, if things go wrong, they send the Astral Knights to sort things out.

You don't want to mess with the Astral Knights. They can blow up planets!

Here on Earth we're known as superheroes. Dad is Captain Valiant. He can fly and has super-strength. He also likes bacon sandwiches and eats lots of them, but that's not really a superpower.

Mum is
Ms Victory. She is
super-clever,
super-fast and tells
Dad off for eating
lots of bacon
sandwiches. She does
all the scientific and
technical stuff.

My sister, Emma,
is Moon Girl.
She can move
objects with her
mind and has a cloak of
invisibility. She is also
very moody and
likes to thump me.

I'm Dynamic Boy. Yes, I know it's a stupid name. But if you think that's stupid, you should see my costume. Dad and Mum look great in red, white and blue. Emma is in black and silver, but looks even better when she's invisible. My costume is black and gold with a lightning  flash down the front. I look like an electric bee. Even my powers aren't much good. All I can do is fly and create illusions. Who cares about that?

When they're not being superheroes, Dad and Mum are Robert and Louise Taylor, IT consultants.

When we're not being superheroes, Emma and I are just two normal children . . . apart from the superpowers, of course. But we're only allowed to use our powers when we're fighting super villains, aliens and all that other nasty stuff. When we're out with our friends we can't use them. When we're at home or school, Mum and Dad want us to be like everyone else. Superpowers are banned, even though Emma and I sometimes use them when we think Mum and Dad won't find out!

We live in a normal house . . . well, almost normal. We have a laboratory hidden under the washing machine in the utility room. That's where we watch out for all those super villains and aliens. I suppose you could call it our secret base, although it's not very big. It's full of computers and strange machines that I don't understand. It's also the place where we go to contact Astral Command – but we only do that in emergencies. We're meant to be able to do this job on our own.

The only thing in the lab that really impresses me is the particle web. It can transport us all over the world in an instant, which is very impressive for something that looks like a giant, green, glowing bogey. At least, *I* think it does. Mum's the only one who really knows how the particle web

works and she doesn't like me calling it a giant, green, glowing bogey. She says it's too important to make fun of. Well, she *is* super-clever, so I suppose she knows what she's talking about.

And that's it really. Apart from fighting

monsters, super villains and protecting the world from alien attacks, we're just a normal family. Of course, we probably have a few more adventures than most normal families and I imagine, if you've read this far, that you're ready for another one.

Well, here it is . . .

CHAPTER 1

Emma was being nice to us. It was Saturday afternoon and we'd just had lunch. We were in the living room. Emma had made Mum and Dad a cup of coffee. She'd brought me a cold drink from the fridge, already poured into a glass. She'd tidied up the kitchen and put all the plates in the dishwasher.

She was also smiling. As she joined us in the living room and sat on the sofa next to Dad, she was actually smiling.

'That was a delicious lunch, Mum,' Emma said. 'Thank you so much. I really do enjoy your tuna and bean salad. You're right when you say healthy food is just as tasty as all those fatty foods which are bad for us.'

I stared at my cold drink as the bubbles fizzed up the side of the glass. I was now convinced that my sister had been abducted by space pirates who were planning to attack the Earth. This person in

front of me was probably a spy sent to find out all she could before the main force arrived.

Dad didn't seem too bothered about sitting next to an impostor. He was still trying to work out how to change the ringtone on his mobile phone. Mum had given us new ones. She'd designed them herself. They were linked to the computers in our lab so that if we received an emergency alert, we'd all know about it at the same time.

Naturally, that meant extra layers of security in case the phones were lost or stolen – that was why Dad couldn't change his ringtone. Now he had to remember two passwords: one to access the phone and one to access all the Astral Guardian stuff.

Dad wasn't good at remembering passwords.

His spelling wasn't that brilliant either, although he said this was because his thumbs were too big for the phone's keypad. 'Louise, what's my password again?' he asked. Dad drank some coffee and put his mug on the arm of the sofa.

Mum picked up a big, hardback book with a title I didn't understand and started to read it. She sat next to me with the book on her knees. She didn't notice Dad's mug on the arm of the sofa. Our suite may have been coffee-coloured but that didn't mean Mum wanted coffee stains on it.

Emma was quick to reach out and put Dad's mug back on the table for him. She then smiled at me and asked, 'Are you all right, Mark? Is there anything I can do for you?'

That was all the proof I needed – whoever this person was, she definitely wasn't my sister!

'Robert,' Mum said, 'your password is *Captain Valiant* followed by your date of birth. I admit it's a bit difficult to remember, but do your best.'

'Right,' Dad said. He sank lower in his seat, concentrating on the phone. He typed the letters one at a time and said them to himself. 'C-A-P-T-A-I-N V-A-L-I-U-N-T.' He pressed the *Enter* key and shook his head. 'No, it doesn't work.'

Emma giggled and playfully slapped Dad's arm. 'Oh, Dad, you're such a tease. I think you may

have made a tiny mistake with your spelling. Valiant is spelt V-A-L-I-*E*-N-T.'

'Is it?' Dad had another go. 'No, that doesn't work either.'

Mum sat back in her seat, closed the book and stared at Emma. I had the feeling she'd come to the same conclusion as me. There was an impostor in the room.

'All right, Emma, much as I appreciate your help with lunch, there has to be a reason for all this . . . niceness. What have you done?'

'Me?' Emma replied. 'I haven't done anything. Why would you think I've done anything?' She sat and beamed at us with a smile so wide it showed all her teeth. 'Would anyone like a chocolate biscuit?'

'Well, if you haven't done anything then you must want something,' Mum said. 'What is it?'

'I don't want anything,' Emma replied. 'No, nothing at all. Honestly, I can't think of a single thing I want, or might want, or could even imagine wanting if I thought about it. No, I have to say I'm very, very happy with everything at the moment.'

She laughed and brushed the arm of the sofa. Her face went the same shade of pink as the curtains.

'Yes, I'm very happy at the moment,' she went on. 'I definitely don't want anything at all . . . Although there is one tiny favour I'd like to ask. It's not much really, just a teeny, tiny favour,

which I'm sure we'd all enjoy.' Her eyes lit up. 'Yes, that's it. It's something we'd all enjoy as a family, something which would help us get to know each other better.' She paused. 'I suppose you know what day it is today?'

'Saturday,' I replied.

'Oh, Mark, you're so funny. I'm so lucky to have a brother as witty as you. No, what I meant is if you know what the date is today.'

So that was it. Mum may have been super-clever but she didn't have to use her superpowers to work out where this conversation was going. Emma had been smart. She hadn't mentioned it for almost a week. 'Emma,' Mum said, 'we're not going to the World Sci-Fi Convention in Las Vegas and that's final.'

'OK,' Emma replied. 'I know that's what you said when I first suggested we should go, and I know that's what you said all the other times I suggested we should go, but it's happening today and they're only about eight hours behind us in Las Vegas, and since we're not really doing anything this afternoon, I thought we could use the particle web and pop over there.'

Mum took a deep breath. 'Emma, I said no and I mean no.'

Emma shot off the sofa. 'That's so unfair!' she shouted. 'Why don't you ever listen to me? I try to be reasonable but, oh no, it's never good enough, is it?

'Go on, give me one good reason why we shouldn't go. And I don't mean any of the reasons you've given me before. All we have to do is beam in, sign a few autographs and beam out again. What's wrong with that?'

'We're Astral Guardians,' Mum said. 'We're not celebrities. We don't give autographs and we don't do guest appearances.'

'I've given autographs,' Dad muttered.

'Well, I hope you spelt your name properly,' Mum said.

Emma knew she couldn't win, that's why she turned to me. She was desperate. 'Mark, you think we should go, don't you?'

Actually, I didn't. This had all started months ago when Emma had been searching the web for articles about Moon Girl. She often did this. Emma liked to know what people were saying about her on the internet, especially when they said something nice. She'd found the homepage of the World Sci-Fi Convention in Las Vegas. It wasn't a very good page and the links didn't work properly, but they'd posted an online invitation for any superhero who wasn't busy saving the world to attend a getting-to-know-you session with the public. To be honest, they sounded a bit desperate to get people to turn up.

'I think I'd prefer to watch football on the telly,' I said.

Emma screamed and kicked the table next to me. My glass fell over and my drink fizzed across the table. It's a good job Mum is super-fast. She had the kitchen roll in her hand and mopped up the mess before anything dripped on the carpet. Mum may not have liked us using our superpowers at home, but there were times when even she broke the rules.

'You're all so boring,' Emma said. 'I don't know why I bother with any of you. I'm so unappreciated.'

Mum dropped the soggy, stained sheets of kitchenroll on the table.

'Right, young lady, that's it.'

Mum pointed at the sheets. 'Go and put that in the bin. I was planning to take you shopping this afternoon, but the way I feel at the moment, I'd like nothing more than to leave you here with your father and brother and go on my own.'

'Please don't,' Dad and I said.

'But why should their afternoon be spoilt by your mood?' Mum went on. 'So whether you like it or not, you're coming with me.'

'I am *not* in a mood,' Emma said. 'And I'm *not* going shopping.'

'Fine.' Mum sat down again. 'I just thought you might want to have a look at that new shop in the high street, you know, the one with that blue dress in the window that you said would look good with those shoes we bought last week.'

Emma folded her arms and huffed. 'Well, I suppose . . . if I don't have a choice. But I'm only going because you've told me to, not because I want to.'

'Louise . . .' Dad said, holding out his phone.

'Robert, your password is *Captain Valiant* followed by your date of birth, and you spell Valiant, V-A-L-I-*A*-N-T. It's not that difficult.'

'I know,' Dad replied. 'The password is fine. It's just that I've received an emergency alert.'

And that's when I heard it – lots of bleeps and bloops coming from my trouser pocket. Emma's and Mum's trousers were making funny noises too. It was the alerts on our phones. We'd been so busy arguing we hadn't heard them! Mum grabbed Dad's phone and read the message on the screen. The look on her face told us all we needed to know. It was time to be superheroes again.

As the four of us made our way down to the lab, Emma said, 'Look, if this emergency doesn't take too long, and it happens to be near Las Vegas, I don't suppose we could fly to the Sci-Fi Convention for just a few minutes, could we?'

CHAPTER 2

It may come as a surprise, but I don't like spaceships very much. I suppose I should. After all, I've been in lots of them. But it doesn't matter how big or small they are, or how fast they fly, spaceships have one basic problem: they're all chunks of metal full of things which can break, fall off or explode.

Spaceships are a bit like cars. When a car gets old or isn't looked after properly it stops working, and when a car breaks down you call someone

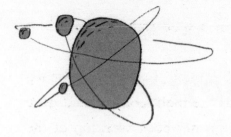

to fix it.
Sometimes,
when a
spaceship breaks
down, and it's

not light years from the nearest planet, you can also call someone to fix it and, on this particular Saturday afternoon, when I should have been watching football, it was Captain Valiant, Ms Victory, Moon Girl and Dynamic Boy who got the call. And that's another reason why I don't like spaceships. They always go wrong at the wrong time.

What was even worse, when we used the particle web to get to this one, it had not only broken down, it was also out of control and on a collision course with Earth. There was only one passenger, the pilot, and he was unconscious on the floor of the flight deck after being hit on the head by a ceiling panel!

Obviously he'd been hit on the head after he'd sent the emergency alert. To be honest, when one thing goes wrong on a spaceship, lots of things go wrong.

Stepping over the pilot, I pulled a heavy electric cable around the flight console and gave it to Mum. She lay on her back working at the console's circuits. She attached wires and unscrewed contacts with her usual super-fast speed. Black smoke and the occasional spark didn't seem to bother her.

I glanced across to where the particle web glowed on the far side of the flight deck. Dad had just gone through it to fetch some equipment from the lab which Mum needed. He'd been getting in her way and she'd told him to go and do something useful. I wished I'd gone with him. I didn't like spending a lot of time on a spaceship that was going to crash.

Emma, who sat in the pilot's chair, swivelled round and poked the unconscious pilot

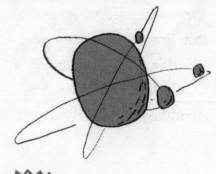

with her foot. She'd only just stopped going on about the Sci-Fi Convention and was now looking for something else to moan about.

'Well, he looks like a criminal to me,' she said. 'He has a scar on his face and he's missing one of his front teeth. If he had an eye patch he'd make a great pirate. And he's not even dressed properly. If he was a pilot he'd wear one of those nice shiny suits, not some brown, tatty overall.'

'Emma, he can't help the way he looks,' Mum said. She handed me a circuit board. 'Mark, check this and tell me if any chips are damaged.' I cried out as the circuit board touched my fingers.

'It's hot,' I said.

'Is it?' Mum glanced at her own fingers. They shone with a clear, oily liquid. 'I wondered what that was. It must be some kind of coolant. Now why has coolant leaked on to the navigation circuits?'

Mum returned her attention to the inside of the flight console. I turned my attention to my stinging fingers. I blew on them while looking round the flight deck and wondered how much longer we had to stay here.

I'd seen some old spaceships before, but this one was an antique. If there was a museum for spaceships, then this would have made a great exhibit. We were in a military shuttle, the kind used for getting troops between planets. The flight deck was small and cramped, not like the modern ones, which had lots of room for the crew to share duties.

The flight console took up most of the floor space. It was a long, rectangular block of grey metal with rows of switches and buttons. Modern

flight consoles had banks of computer terminals with hand sensors and fingertip controls. The walls and ceiling were also made of the same grey metal as the console. Some of the panels had fallen out and showed tangled knots of charred wires.

Of course, the metal might not have been grey. When we stepped out of the particle web, I noticed my footprints on the floor as I walked across it. The flight deck was so filthy, the metal could have been white and the grey colour caused by all the dust and dirt.

It was also warm – too warm to be

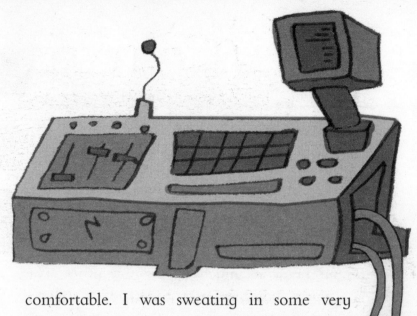

comfortable. I was sweating in some very embarrassing places. I suppose the heat had something to do with whatever had gone wrong. Mum had said the coolant was leaking, but it was such a small flight deck and full of so much electrical equipment I was certain it would have been warm even if there wasn't a problem with the cooling systems.

It felt like I was stuck in an oven, being slowly roasted. The sooner I got back to sitting in front of the television with a cold drink, the better.

'He could have been lying,' Emma said, prodding the pilot again. 'I mean, anyone can send an emergency alert. Don't get me wrong, it's obvious the ship is damaged. But what caused the damage? That's what I want to know. Maybe he's on the run. Maybe he's been in a battle with another ship and he's trying to escape before they blast him to bits.'

Mum said nothing. We'd all been in the lab when she'd played back the emergency alert. Emma knew as much as the rest of us. The message was very garbled, probably because the damage to the ship had affected the transmission.

All we knew for certain was that the pilot claimed to be an agent with the Bureau of Undercover Research Personnel. The BURP was an interplanetary security firm, which specialised in gathering information about potential threats

to the galaxy. During our Astral Guardian training they ran a course on encryption and code breaking. It was very boring.

This agent, Vallen Pohl, had said he was on a mission of galactic importance that had something to do with a weapon  called the Eternity Stone. Then the message had broken up and we couldn't make any more sense of it. Our scanners tracked his ship on its way to Earth but, as far as we could tell, there was no other ship close enough to help him. It was up to us.

'And since he *is* a spy,' Emma went on, 'and since he *does* work for the BURP, he'd be very good at lying.'

'He's not a spy,' Mum replied. 'His official title is Private Order Operative.'

'All right, so he's a POO who works for the BURP. Either way, he's still probably involved in something secretive and dangerous.' Emma stared at Pohl. 'If you want my opinion, I don't think we should trust him. This all smells a bit fishy to me.'

'Well, if he's a POO, it would smell more than a bit fishy,' I muttered.

Emma glowered at me. 'I've decided you're not funny any more,' she said. 'Why don't you get back to burning your fingers or whatever it is you're doing?'

'For your information,' I replied, 'I'm helping to fix this ship. Why don't you do something a bit more useful than sitting on your backside staring at the POO?'

'Excuse me,' Emma said, leaning on the flight console, 'but which one of us is holding up the ceiling with her thoughts?' She stretched out her hands. 'You don't seriously think I'm going to get these dirty when I have the power to move objects with my mind?'

I hated to admit it, but she was right. Emma's job was to make sure none of us were injured by more falling panels. No one cared about her clean hands, but we all cared about getting hit on the head by chunks of metal.

'Louise?' Dad said, stepping out of the particle web. 'Is this the one you wanted?'

Mum looked up from the console. 'Robert,' she said, 'I asked you to bring the automatic electron stabiliser, not the manual particle agitator.'

Dad looked at the long metal rod in his hands. It had a pointed end, a dial in the middle and a red handle with buttons on the grip. He had the same expression on his face as when he'd tried to enter the password on his phone.

'It was the short thing in the cupboard next to that one,' Mum said. 'You know . . . with the blue handle.'

'Oh, sorry.' Dad glanced back at the particle web. 'I'll go and —'

'No, it's all right, I'll do it myself.' Mum stood up. 'I know what the problem is now. It shouldn't take long to fix. I've managed to reset the navigation control so we won't crash into Earth, but I still need to repair the booster circuits. I'll go back to the lab and get what I need.' She looked at the unconscious pilot.

'And when that's
done, I'll have
a few questions to
ask Vallen Pohl.
He may be a BURP
agent and he may be
one of the good guys, but that doesn't mean he's
told us the whole truth. Robert, you stay and
watch him. Emma, you stay and make sure the
ship doesn't fall apart. Mark, you come with me
and help bring back the *right* equipment this
time.'

'You see?' Emma said, spinning round on the
pilot's seat. 'I told you he was involved in
something secretive and dangerous.'

'Of course he is,' Mum replied. 'That's why I
want to know exactly what's going on.'

Mum stepped into the particle web and
disappeared. I was about to follow her when the
ship gave a sudden jolt. Dad lost his balance and
crashed into the wall. I grabbed hold of the
flight console and swore out loud as my burnt

fingers scraped across the metal. Emma made a strange yowling noise and ended up sprawled across Pohl.

But that wasn't the worst of it. As the jolt went through the ship, the particle web vanished. I didn't know why it vanished. All I knew for certain was that it shouldn't have. The web was our only way home. There were loads of safety protocols so I was sure Mum had made it back to the lab OK, but what about us? We were now completely alone without the one person who knew how to fix the spaceship. I knew Mum would get the particle web working again, but what else might go wrong in the time it took her to repair it?

And we had another problem. There was a high-pitched

It came from above us, as if something was clawing at the hull. Emma, Dad and I stared at the ceiling. I think we all expected something to burst through. Instead, the screech stopped and the ship gave a second, less violent, jolt. Then I had the strangest feeling of upward movement, like I was in a lift.

'Oh great,' a croaking voice said, 'you've found me.'

It was Pohl. Using the flight console for support, he struggled to his feet and sat in the pilot's seat. He groaned and rubbed his head. His fingers left a smear of blood on his brow. Pohl saw the blood and smiled as if it reminded him of something. The scar on his cheek went white against his smoke-stained face.

'You must be Astral Guardians,' he said. 'I wasn't sure if my alert got through.' He glanced round the flight deck. 'So where's the particle web? I thought that's how you people went from place to place.'

A hammering echoed through the ship. There was no doubt about it now – something or someone was definitely trying to get inside.

'Oh, that's not good,' Pohl said. 'I thought it would take them longer to find me. Well, that plan didn't work, did it? Now they'll get the Eternity Stone back and it'll be over for all of us. But we almost saved the galaxy, didn't we? Unfortunately, almost saving the galaxy isn't as good as actually saving it.'

Sparks exploded from the ceiling. The glare was so bright I had to look away. Someone was cutting through the hull with a laser.

'If you want my advice,' Pohl shouted over the hiss of the sparks, 'don't tell them anything about the Eternity Stone. If you do, they'll probably kill you. After all, if you plan to conquer the galaxy, you don't want anyone to know you have a secret weapon until it's too late to do anything about it!'

CHAPTER 3

When the sparks faded, there was a

A square section of metal was lifted out of the ceiling and four men's faces stared down at us. The faces weren't friendly. It would have been much easier to know why they weren't friendly if we'd all spoken the same language, but the men who stood on the edge of the hole didn't speak English and I didn't understand a word of what they said.

But I didn't need to understand. Their guns did most of the talking. Orders are a bit easier to follow when they're given at the point of a gun.

A ladder dropped down and we climbed up one by one. When we got to the top, there were six guards waiting for us. They were dressed in military uniforms and they all had guns – big, heavy guns with lots of red flashing lights. Dad, Emma and I were marched off in one direction while Pohl was taken in another. Two guards pushed and shoved him down a narrow corridor, helping him on his way with an occasional punch to the stomach or face.

'I hope that's not their way of making someone feel welcome,' Emma said.

I went to reply but Dad glared at me. I could tell he wanted us to be quiet. The guards may not have spoken English but that didn't mean they couldn't understand what we were saying, and if we said anything about Pohl or this thing called the Eternity Stone, we might end up in a lot more trouble than we were already.

And we were in a lot of trouble. Our little spaceship had been pulled into the hold of the biggest battle cruiser I'd ever seen – probably by a force field or a magnetic locking beam. The cruiser was so large, the hold in which we stood had trucks to carry crates, and cranes to lift metal

containers the size of train carriages. There were at least three more decks above me and a maze of gantries and walkways between them. Men and women in oil-stained overalls operated huge machines which hissed and rumbled. There must have been hundreds of people at work on our deck alone.

'Now this is a big ship,' Emma said. She nudged me. 'How big do you think it is?'

'Big enough,' I replied.

'Yes, but how big?'

I shrugged. 'Big enough not to ask questions about how big it is.'

A guard chuckled. There were two in front and two behind us. We'd followed a walkway marked with yellow lines between two huge walls of green storage compartments. Not one of them had spoken since we'd come onboard, so when the guard laughed, either he'd thought of something funny or he'd understood what I'd said – and he didn't look like the kind of man who had funny thoughts jumping around inside his head.

We came to a crossroads. Across from us, the storage compartments ended and were replaced by rows and rows of guns and blasters. There were enough weapons to arm hundreds, if not

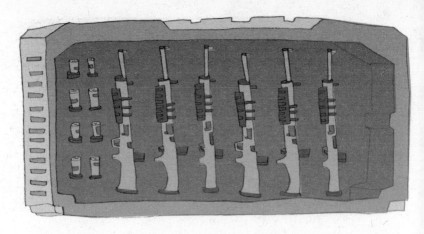

thousands, of soldiers. Even though we were superheroes, we wouldn't be able to put up much of a fight against an army with all that firepower. Whatever we'd got mixed up in, this definitely wasn't the time or place to think about trying to escape or rescuing a BURP agent.

For some reason the guards stopped. There

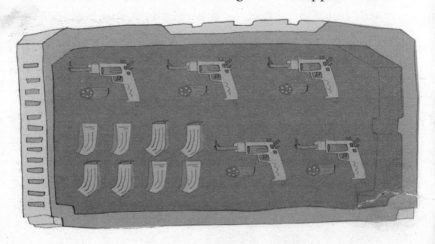

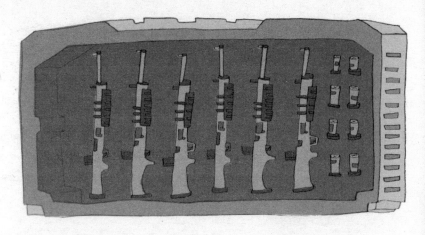

was nothing blocking our way, but they remained motionless and silent. Emma leant forward and looked to the left and right. A guard pushed her back.

'What's happening?' she asked.

Dad put his hand on her shoulder and his finger to his lips. 'Listen,' he said.

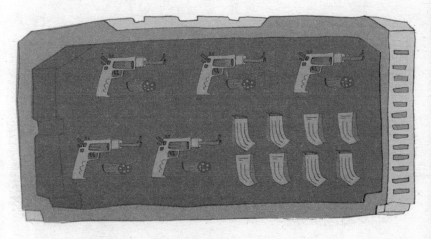

That's when I heard it – a strange, metal clanging. Trying not to attract the attention of the guards or Dad, I also leant forward and looked to the left and right.

They came towards us in rows of three with slow, steady steps. Each one was twice the height of a man and as wide as a car. They had four legs, a rectangular body and a triangular head.

The lights in the hold reflected off their metal bodies, which were polished so brightly it was like looking in a mirror. A point on the triangular head formed a snout, and below the snout was a jointed jaw with metal teeth. On either side of the snout was a small black dome, like a pair of eyes.

The machines, whatever they were, reminded

me of wolves. They didn't seem to have drivers inside them and they moved in time with each other, their metal feet ringing against the floor. Even though my eyes and ears told me that these things were mechanical, it was as if I was looking at living creatures.

Now, I may have superpowers and I may have fought a lot of super villains, but when I saw these wolves, I felt completely powerless. They were obviously some kind of weapon. I just hoped it was a weapon I never had to fight. There was something about those triangular heads with their metal teeth and black eyes that made me shudder. Once the wolves passed – and it took a long time for them to pass since there must have been over two hundred of them – the guards moved on again. As we went over the crossroads, the guard nearest Dad slipped and fell. He'd stepped in a patch of oil left behind by one of the wolves. The machine must have sprung a leak.

'You know, if you're going to have pets,' I said, walking round the guard, 'you really should make sure they're house-trained.'

We didn't see anything as impressive, or frightening, after that. There were more technicians and a lot more soldiers. We walked through a cargo bay with snaking lines of orange trucks and came to a set of double doors.

It was here that our guards left us – after they'd typed a code into a keypad, waited until the doors opened and used their guns to force us through. We found ourselves in a squat cylinder. It was a lift and we were going up. When the doors opened again, I expected there to be more guards waiting. There weren't.

Instead, we stared out at rows and rows of

uniformed men and women who worked at consoles and monitors. There was a low murmur of conversation and lots of clicks and clacks as fingers tapped at keypads and light pens scribbled on screens.

'This must be the main control room,' Dad said.

'It's definitely somewhere important,' I replied.

'I don't care what it is,' Emma said. 'I bet you wish we were at a Sci-Fi Convention now.'

CHAPTER 4

At the front of the control room, taking up most of the wall, was a huge screen that showed a picture of Earth. The planet's bright glare gave off a pale blue haze. Standing on a raised platform overlooking the room, silhouetted by the haze, was a woman. She stared at the Earth with her arms folded across her chest.

A man crossed to the bottom of the steps that led up to the platform. He said something and the woman turned. After glancing in our direction, she dismissed the man with a nod and made her way down to us.

It wasn't difficult to work out that this woman was in charge. She walked with the confidence of someone who was used to giving orders. Her face was long and straight with high cheekbones. Her blond hair had been cut so short she might as well have shaved it off. She was as tall as Dad but very thin. I wondered how long it had been since she'd had a good meal.

The woman stopped a little way from the lift and smiled. The smile didn't suit her face.

'I am Commander Dorian,' the woman said. 'And you must be Captain Valiant, Moon Girl and Dynamic Boy.' She stared at each one of us in turn. 'Please, won't you come in?' A hand with long, bony fingers invited us to join her.

We didn't move. I don't know why Dad and Emma stayed where they were, but I stayed where I was because, as I met Commander Dorian's gaze, it felt like I was staring straight into the eyes of one of those huge, metal wolves.

Commander Dorian frowned and scowled. Not only was she a woman who was used to giving orders, it seemed she was also a woman used to having those orders obeyed.

She gave a single, harsh snap of her fingers and a guard with a gun appeared at the lift doors.

'Captain Valiant,' Commander

Dorian said, 'although English isn't my first language, I am able to communicate well enough for you to understand me. Now, since I do not like to repeat myself, please explain why you are still in the lift.'

Dad led us out. The doors closed without a

sound. While Dad kept his eyes on Commander Dorian, Emma and I looked around the control room.

It was a high-ceilinged hexagon with a gallery just below the roof. Two flights of stairs on either side led up to the gallery and a constant stream of people went up and down them. Like everything else I'd seen on the ship, the control room was practical rather than pretty. Most of the space was taken up with technical equipment. There was nothing remarkable about the room – apart from its size and the number of crew and, of course, the line of armed guards who stood directly above us on the gallery.

I didn't count them. I didn't need to. They had enough guns pointed at us to make sure I wasn't too curious. It seemed Commander Dorian was expecting trouble.

'So you must be Astral Guardians,' she said. 'The Astral Command planetary incident log only gave basic information about the team it had assigned to Earth. But even so, there are four

of you listed.
Where is . . .'
She thought for
a moment.
'. . . Ms Victory?'
Dad shrugged.

'She wanted to look her best and went home to change.'

Commander Dorian wasn't amused.

'Captain Valiant,' she said, 'do you feel humour is appropriate at a time like this? Well, if you want to tell jokes, I shall have to find something we'll all find funny.' She summoned a guard and spoke to him in her own language. The guard marched out of the room. She then summoned one of the crew and also gave him an order. 'But I shouldn't expect you to take this seriously. You are nothing more than what you appear to be. Now what's the word for it . . . ? Ah, yes, "clowns". You dress like clowns and act like clowns. It really is hard to believe that Astral Command trusts clowns to protect a planet. At least the FART takes its responsibilities seriously.'

You know, there are times when you think you've heard something, but it sounds so silly that you tell yourself you couldn't have heard it.

Emma must have thought the same.

'Did she say the FART take their responsibilities seriously?' she whispered.

'Yes, that's exactly what I said,' Commander Dorian snapped. 'The FART takes its responsibilities very seriously.'

'And who are the FART?' Emma asked.

Commander Dorian looked surprised. '*We* are the FART.' She indicated the room with a flick of her hand. 'You are on the battle cruiser X1, the biggest and most powerful ship in the FART fleet. I am the Senior FART Commander for this sector of galaxy, and you,' she pointed at us, 'are my prisoners. You stand accused of trying to steal

the Eternity Stone, the most powerful FART weapon ever created. It is a crime punishable by death. The Federal Army of the Republic of Taranos shows no leniency to those who steal its property.'

I'm sure this would have sounded a lot more frightening if I hadn't been trying to make sense of what had actually happened to us. So we'd tried to help a POO who worked for the BURP and now we were prisoners of the FART?

This was definitely going to cause a stink at Astral Command!

Dad, who was finding it difficult not to laugh, coughed back a snigger.

'Commander Dorian,' he said, 'I'm afraid you've got it wrong. We haven't stolen anything. We're Astral Guardians, not thieves.'

'And yet, Captain, you were caught on the same spaceship as the man who stole the Eternity Stone. One way or another, you are involved in the theft. The man's name, as I'm sure you know, is Vallen Pohl, and he was an engineer on the X1. With the help of others in my crew – whose identities will soon be known to me – he took the Eternity Stone and headed for Earth in a spaceship which had been scheduled to be scrapped. Now, not only do I believe Pohl had a team working on the X1, but I also suspect he was going to meet someone on Earth and pass the Eternity Stone on to them. Of course, I had no idea his contacts would be Astral Guardians - not that it makes a difference. Once I find out the identity of *all* those involved I will deal with you all severely.'

The guard who had marched out of the room now returned. He carried a large, white box which he put on the floor in front of Commander Dorian. Behind him, two more guards appeared. They carried Vallen Pohl. The BURP agent had a lot more blood on his face than when I'd last seen him.

Commander Dorian paid no attention to Pohl. She grinned like a child about to open a present. She bent down and stroked the top of the box.

'I expect you saw some of the weapons the FART have developed on your way up here,' she said, laying her hand on the lid. The white colour faded so that the contents of the box could be seen. 'But not all our weapons are mechanical. Some are living things — beautiful, living, crawling things which are just as deadly as everything else we make.'

Inside the box, filling it up to about half its depth, was a heaving, writhing, squirming lump of bright red slugs. They slid and slithered up the sides. It made me queasy just to look at them.

I didn't see her move but I felt Emma stand close to me. Her hand briefly touched mine. Dad stood between us and the box,

although we could still see what Commander Dorian was doing.

'They have a technical name,' Dorian said, 'but it's very long and boring. I call them brain leeches. We use them to get people to tell us what we want to know.' She opened the lid, reached into the box and picked up a leech. She held it between her fingers. The leech jerked and twisted in her grip. 'All you do is insert one of these into a person's body, either through the nose, the mouth or . . .' She laughed. '. . . anywhere the leech can find a way in. Once it's inside, the leech finds a warm place to feed and, while feeding, it injects a chemical into the bloodstream which makes it impossible for a person to tell lies. Naturally, there's a small side effect. The chemical is an acid.

Within days a person melts from the inside. It's a very unpleasant way to die.'

She looked at the leech.

'On the other hand, these things do make a rather tasty snack.' She lifted the leech to her mouth and bit it in two. A blob of yellow gunge spilt on her lips. 'They're a bit spicy but you get used to the taste after a while.'

She dropped the other half in her mouth. 'You also have to make sure you kill them with the first bite, otherwise, if one of them gets down your throat and it's still alive . . . well, you know the rest.'

I hadn't noticed it before, but a familiar green glow now shone at the back of the control room near the lift. I knew what it was and a part of me wished it wasn't there. I wanted to shout a warning, only it wouldn't have made a difference.

Mum stepped out of the particle web.

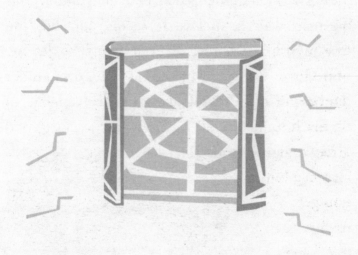

Commander Dorian wiped the yellow gunge from her lips and barked an order in her own language. The particle web vanished.

Great! When I saw the particle web, I thought we might have a chance to escape. Now, even though Mum was here, we were no better off!

'Ah, Ms Victory,' Dorian said, 'I'm so glad you've joined us. Welcome aboard the X1. I knew if I deactivated our defence shields your scanners would pick us up and you'd be able to use the particle web to get here. But, as you can see, now that I've ordered them to be activated again, your particle web is useless. It seems you are my prisoner, like the rest of your team. So let me introduce myself. My name is Commander Dorian of the Federal Army of the Republic of Taranos and I will be your judge, jury and executioner for today.'

CHAPTER 5

Despite still being trapped by the FART, I was very glad to see Mum. I think we all were. I heard Emma mutter, 'And about time too,' while Dad smiled and clenched his fists. Of course, we would all have been a bit happier if the particle web hadn't vanished. But still, if anyone could think of a way to get us home, then it was Mum.

Commander Dorian glanced at the leeches in the box. One of them had crawled over the top and fallen to the floor. It wriggled its way towards her boot. She stamped on it.

'Well, now you're all here,' she said, 'we can begin. Would anyone like to go first?'

Mum ignored Commander Dorian. She walked over to us.

'Is everyone all right?' she asked. 'Is anyone hurt?'

'Only Pohl,' I said.

Mum looked over her shoulder at the limp figure of the BURP agent. He really was in a bad way. He seemed to be unconscious. Blood dripped from his nose and mouth down his tatty, brown overalls.

'Don't worry about Pohl,' Mum said. 'He can take care of himself.'

'Really?' I replied. 'It doesn't look like that to me.'

Mum turned to face Commander Dorian. 'Well, Commander,' she said, 'since you are to be my judge, jury and executioner, may I ask what crime I've been accused of committing?'

'We're accused of helping Pohl steal something

called the Eternity Stone,' Dad said. 'I told her we know nothing about it, but she's convinced we're involved and is going to use those leeches to prove it.'

Mum didn't appear to listen. She approached Commander Dorian.

'You realise you have exceeded your authority, don't you, Commander?' she said. 'I have some knowledge of the rules and regulations

concerning the treatment of prisoners by the Federal Army of the Republic of Taranos. Even under FART law, we are entitled to a fair trial.'

'No, Ms Victory,' Commander Dorian replied. 'As the supreme authority aboard this ship, I may interpret those rules as I see fit. You are entitled to nothing but my judgement; and my judgement has found you guilty as charged. All I require now are the full details of your guilt and the names of everyone involved.'

Another leech crawled out of the box. Once again, Commander Dorian crushed it underfoot. She scraped her boot across the floor, leaving a long, red and yellow smear.

'Then if we can't have a fair trial,' Mum said, 'can we at least see what we are accused of stealing?'

Commander Dorian laughed and shouted an order in her own language.

'Of course you can, Ms Victory,' she said. 'Since there is no possibility of you being able to steal the Eternity Stone again, I would like nothing more than for you to have another look at the object which will be the cause of your miserable deaths. It is only fitting that you should see it before the leeches go to work.'

Commander Dorian leant close to Mum and lowered her voice.

'On the other hand, I am curious. I know that you must be planning some way of escape. If I were in your position, I would certainly be planning some way of escape. I'd like you to try, I really would. It's no fun when someone gives up without a fight. I want you to do whatever it is you do in those ridiculous costumes. Astral Guardians are supposed to have special powers, aren't they? Go on, make it interesting. Threaten me, attack me, do something brave and heroic just so that I can see the look on your face when I crush you like one of these leeches.'

Dorian got so close to Mum their noses almost touched.

'Because I'm going to teach you an important lesson today, Ms Victory – the last lesson you'll

74

ever learn. I'm going to teach you that courage is nothing compared to ruthlessness.'

A guard ran forward. He held a small, silver cylinder, which he offered to Commander Dorian.

'No,' she said, 'give it to her while she still believes she has a chance to win this fight.'

The guard did as he was ordered. Mum took

the cylinder and, without hesitation, twisted the ends. The cylinder clicked open and, from a small compartment in the middle, a blue light shone. I tried to see what caused the light. It looked like a small, black cube – about the size of a matchbox – and, even though it was solid black, it still glowed with blue light. Mum closed the cylinder quickly.

'Beautiful, isn't it?' Commander Dorian said. 'I think that's why they call it the Eternity Stone. When you look at it you get a sense of . . . oh, I don't know . . . the limitless power it contains. You should consider yourself fortunate, Ms Victory. What you have there is the only one of its kind. The Stone has taken decades to develop. We've been conducting the final tests on it. When we return to Taranos, this stone – the ultimate FART weapon – goes into full production. Every ship in our fleet will be equipped with one. I have to say, it has exceeded all our expectations – a device which destroys without leaving behind any evidence. You may find this hard to believe, but I have just obliterated an entire planet. It was only a chunk of rock, no bigger than the Earth, but there is nothing left of it, not even a speck of dust.

Think what you could do with such a weapon, Ms Victory. You could wipe out armies, cities, whole civilisations before anyone realised you had declared war.'

Mum's grip tightened on the cylinder. 'Actually, this device doesn't destroy anything,' she said. 'If I'm right, it's a quark imploder. It reduces matter to its basic subatomic elements and then converts those elements to light. The planet you think you destroyed was actually converted into energy and stored in this.' Mum held up the cylinder. 'I've read research papers on quark implosion but I never thought I'd see a working device.'

'Really?' Commander Dorian snatched the cylinder from Mum. 'Well, I'm so pleased I've satisfied your academic curiosity. Now, where are those leeches?'

They were all over the floor, or at least quite a few of them were. Some of the crew had even stopped working and were looking anxiously around as the leeches wriggled out of the box.

'Mark,' Mum said, pointing at my foot. 'Perhaps you should do something about that.'

I looked down and saw a leech squirming over my toe. I flicked it off and went to stamp on it.

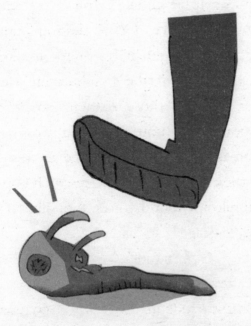

'No, Mark, that's not what I meant,' Mum said. 'Even something as ugly as a leech can be useful, if you know how to use it properly.'

And then I understood what Mum wanted me to do. I had no idea what her plan was, but I didn't doubt her for a minute. We were Astral Guardians. We were a team. This is what we did – we fought back when it seemed impossible to win.

And that's when the screaming started.

CHAPTER 6

It was the guard who'd brought in the box of leeches who screamed first. Well, it wasn't so much a scream as a high-pitched gurgle, but it still got everyone's attention. Using my power to create illusions, I'd made a leech appear on his cheek, just under his eye. The man smacked it away, staggered back, tripped and fell.

He landed with a squelch on a floor now covered in leeches. Some of them were real but most of them were illusion. There were certainly

far more
than could
have fitted in
the box, but
that didn't
matter. The
fact that the
guard was
scared meant that he wasn't thinking clearly. He
thrashed around in a puddle of squashed leeches,
howling and bellowing like a wounded animal.

The guards on the gallery also made a lot of
strange noises. Guns clattered to the floor as I
made more leeches drop from the ceiling on to
their hands and necks. There were so many of
the red, glistening blobs that it seemed to be
raining blood.

The crew of the control room didn't escape the
confusion. Leeches crawled from behind
computer screens and popped out from under
chairs. Men and women shot out of their seats

with leeches in their laps. People clawed at their hair, pulled leeches out of their noses or spat them out of their mouths. Some people tore at their clothes, pulling off shirts and trousers as leeches slithered through zips and in-between buttons.

It was all a bit embarrassing really. Watching people in their underwear standing on desks, shouting and screaming, isn't that funny. One man had gone so far as to take all his clothes off. He bolted for the stairs to the gallery and dashed up them, tripping and stumbling. He disappeared through the door at the top with a wailing cry.

The only member of the crew who wasn't fooled by the illusions was Commander Dorian. She stood and watched as everyone went wild around her. She didn't even shout an order. Instead, a smile spread across her face. 'Well,' she said, 'I didn't expect that.' 'Robert,' Mum shouted, 'get Pohl!'

FLICK!

Dad did as he was told. The guards who'd brought Pohl on to the flight deck had already let him go. They were too busy squashing leeches to worry about a bruised and battered BURP agent. Pohl couldn't stand on his own and had collapsed. Dad had to pick him up off the floor.

'Emma,' Mum shouted again, 'take this, turn invisible and stay close to me!' She threw the Eternity Stone to Emma. She must have used her

super-speed to snatch it from Commander Dorian. Seeing the silver cylinder disappear from her hands, fly through the air and vanish as Emma pulled up her hood, Commander Dorian's smile turned into a snarl. She dashed across to the nearest guard and grabbed a gun. She aimed it at the spot where Emma stood.

Thankfully, Commander Dorian didn't get a chance to shoot. Dad strode past her with Pohl under one arm and wrenched the gun out of her hands. He threw the gun across the room, picked up Commander Dorian by the collar and dropped her, bottom first, into the box of leeches.

'I hope you were wrong about those things finding any way they can into a person's body,' Dad said, 'because if you're not, you're going to be very uncomfortable, very soon.'

Commander Dorian growled and grunted and tried to get up, but her backside was wedged in the box. She had to roll over and crawl across the floor with the box stuck on her bottom. She bellowed at the guards to pull the box off, only

they were too busy pulling the imaginary leeches off their own bodies.

'Right everyone,' Mum yelled, 'get over here now!' She was inside the lift at the back of the control room, pulling wires out of a wall panel. 'Once these doors close they won't open again until we get to the loading bays!'

Dad and I ran inside. Propping Pohl against the wall, Dad faced the flight deck in case anyone came after us. They didn't. The doors closed quickly and the lift went down so fast that

I lost my balance and fell against Emma. She pushed me away and I stumbled into Pohl. He slid to the floor. Looking down at him, I realised just how badly he'd been beaten. His face was so swollen and bloody it was almost unrecognisable.

'Now listen, all of you,' Mum said. 'As soon as Commander Dorian gets control of her crew again, she'll alert the rest of the ship to our escape. There will probably be guards waiting for us when these doors open. Mark, make it look like we're technicians. Robert, when the doors open, you and I will deal with the guards before they work out who we really are. Emma, take care of Pohl. Keep him upright with your thoughts, stay invisible and hold on to the Eternity Stone.' I did what Mum told

me to do and made
us look like ship's
technicians.
The lift stopped and
the doors opened.
Mum was right.
There were three
guards waiting for us.

The guards didn't
move. In fact, they
didn't seem to know
what to do. One of
them came forward
and shouted something in his own language. He
was taller and broader than the others. His stern
look and sharp tone made me think he was in
charge. Dad was about to leap out at him when
the guard spun round and shot the others who
stood behind him. Their bodies disappeared in a
cloud of ash and smoke.

The guard faced us again. 'You must be the
Astral Guardians,' he said. 'Commander Dorian

said you were on your
way down from the
control room. If I'm right,
show me who you really
are. Because if you're not
Astral Guardians . . .'

His gun rose.

Mum told me to end the illusion.

'I'm with the BURP,' the guard said, lowering
his gun. 'My name is Brunner. I'm part of the
team assigned to steal the Eternity Stone.' He
glanced at Pohl. 'Do you have it?'

Mum said nothing. Brunner offered his gun to
her.

'I've just killed two guards,' he said. 'If you
don't believe I'm a BURP agent,
shoot me and find your
own way off this ship.'

Mum took the gun. She
looked at it carefully and
then fired a single blast

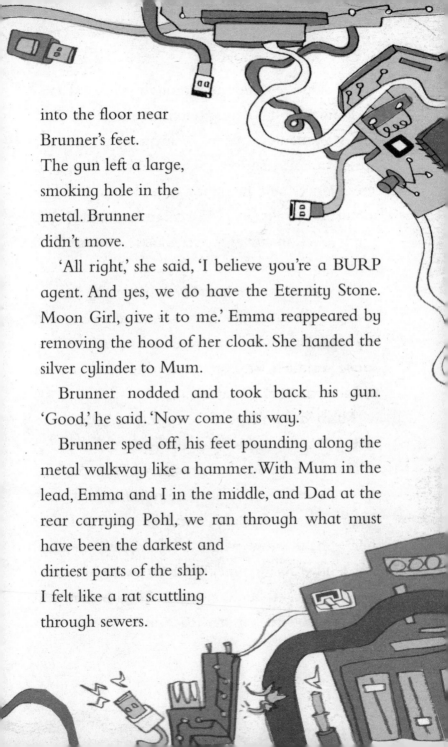

into the floor near Brunner's feet. The gun left a large, smoking hole in the metal. Brunner didn't move.

'All right,' she said, 'I believe you're a BURP agent. And yes, we do have the Eternity Stone. Moon Girl, give it to me.' Emma reappeared by removing the hood of her cloak. She handed the silver cylinder to Mum.

Brunner nodded and took back his gun. 'Good,' he said. 'Now come this way.'

Brunner sped off, his feet pounding along the metal walkway like a hammer. With Mum in the lead, Emma and I in the middle, and Dad at the rear carrying Pohl, we ran through what must have been the darkest and dirtiest parts of the ship. I felt like a rat scuttling through sewers.

We didn't see anyone although we heard lots of clanging and banging and the echo of muffled voices. Sometimes we were in more danger of being strangled by loose wires or being knocked out by overhanging pipes than being shot or captured. Finally, when it seemed as if we'd been going round in circles, we reached a small, square door which Brunner kicked open.

We jumped into a long room, which had rows of tall, silver tubes along its sides. Each tube was big enough to fit one person and each one opened at the front. Inside, the tubes were padded with black, spongy material.

'These are emergency escape pods,' Brunner said, going to a console at the end of the room. 'The other members of our team have made sure they can only be controlled from this room. Once they're launched, Dorian will be able to track them. She'll know where you're going, so you won't have much time. We'll do everything we can to prevent her coming after you, but we won't be able to stop her for long.'

Brunner stood at the console and pushed buttons. Lights came on above the tubes and I heard a low hum.

'All you need to do is get the Eternity Stone to Pohl's contact on Earth,' Brunner said. 'Pohl can't complete his mission, but you're Astral Guardians – you can do it for him. After all, we're on the same side, aren't we? I'm sure Astral Command wouldn't mind if you helped the BURP steal the Eternity Stone.'

I could tell Mum wasn't happy about getting involved in a BURP mission. I suppose I understood why. Usually it was Mum who told us what to do. After all, she *was* super-clever, and it's always a good idea to let the person who knows what they're talking about give the orders. Mum indicated that we should stay where we were and went to speak to Brunner. There was a lot of head shaking and finger pointing. Mum did most of the finger pointing and Brunner did most of the head shaking. When she came back, it was clear

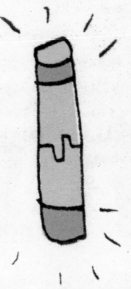

that the finger pointing hadn't made a difference. We were going to do what the BURP wanted whether we liked it or not.

'Robert,' Mum said, 'leave Pohl here.'

Dad lowered Pohl to the floor. The man didn't make a sound. I wasn't even sure he was still breathing.

'I've programmed the pods to take you to where Pohl planned to meet his contact,' Brunner said. 'The contact is another BURP agent who has already been advised of the situation up here. The location for the meeting is a city called Las Vegas in the Nevada Desert in North America. Do you know it?'

Mum closed her eyes and gritted her teeth. Dad shook his head and muttered something under his breath. Emma and I looked at each other.

'I've changed my mind,' Emma said. 'I don't want to go to Las Vegas any more. Can't we go shopping instead?'

CHAPTER 7

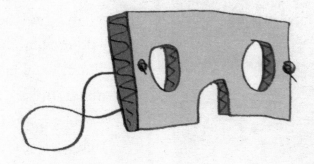

Shopping sounded like a good idea to me. It sounded an even better idea as I climbed into my pod and settled into the black, spongy material. As soon as the pod closed, I was in complete darkness. I couldn't see anything, hear anything or feel anything except the black, spongy stuff. It was like floating in warm jelly.

And that was it. I waited for something to happen. I stared into the darkness expecting the pod to vibrate or shake. It didn't. In fact, everything

was so quiet and dark, I thought the pod wasn't working properly. I tried to reach the door, only my hands wouldn't move. In fact, I couldn't move any part of my body except my eyes and mouth. The black stuff held me down like glue. I didn't panic. After all, this was an escape pod. It was designed to keep someone safe as

they shot through space.
But still, it would have
made the darkness and
the silence a bit more
bearable if I'd known for certain
that I *was* shooting through space.

So when the doors opened and light poured into the pod, I thought I must still be on the X1. I'd only been in the dark for a few minutes.

'Come on, Mark, get up.'

It was Dad. He reached into the pod and hammered at the black, spongy stuff, which had now become hard and brittle. It broke easily and I was soon standing in the open air, brushing myself down. Mum and Emma stood beside their own pods, flicking black bits from their costumes.

'Well, here we are, then,' Dad said. He put his hands on his hips and stared out at the horizon. 'You know, if I was going to meet a secret agent at a secret location and hand over a secret weapon, I'd have chosen somewhere a bit more secret than this.'

I followed Dad's stare. A hot, harsh wind blew in my face. It scratched my cheeks and stung my eyes. I had to blink to focus on what was in front of me – the parched sand and rock of the Nevada Desert and, about ten minutes' walk from where I stood, overshadowed by the glittering steel and glass of Las Vegas, the World Sci-Fi Convention.

Despite its name, the World Sci-Fi Convention

wasn't very impressive. Sagging banners and faded flags decorated the tops of dingy marquees and shabby exhibition halls. There were lots of people walking around and lots of signs advertising different events, but the whole thing looked a bit disorganised and ramshackle. Even the sci-fi fans looked a bit threadbare. There was the usual array of bright costumes and painted

faces, but the tin foil and the rubber masks seemed more of a joke than a serious attempt to look like anything alien or scary.

'Actually,' Mum said, 'this is the perfect place for a secret meeting. I expect the BURP's original plan was for Pohl to land, destroy his ship and then meet up with his contact. With so many people in so many costumes, they wouldn't be noticed. The BURP are very good at this kind of thing. Every detail would have been thought through carefully.'

'Then why did it all go wrong?' Emma asked.

Mum thought for a few moments. 'I don't know,' she said. 'Maybe it was just bad luck.'

The wind hit me in the face again. A crumpled crisp packet skidded across the sand and an empty bottle of mineral water rolled against my foot. I heard the rumble of engines, the clunk of car doors and the twitter of excited children.

'I don't suppose anyone has a pen?' Emma asked. 'You know, just in case, someone . . . well, you know, recognises us or something.' She straightened her costume, tidied her hair and put on the mask she had to wear when she could be seen in public. 'After all, it would be a shame not to sign a few autographs. We can't upset our fans.'

'I wouldn't worry about autographs or fans,' Mum said. 'We're going to pretend we're just another family of sci-fi enthusiasts. Under no circumstances are any of us to use our powers unless I say so. We must act like ordinary people. Our first concern is the Eternity Stone. We have to pass it on to our contact before Commander Dorian comes after us.'

'Really?' Emma pointed at the escape pods. 'Well, maybe if we're supposed to be an ordinary family, we shouldn't have dropped out of

the sky in four silver tubes. Most ordinary families drive cars.'

Mum walked past Emma and headed for the Convention. 'Those escape pods were made by the FART,' she said. 'They wouldn't have been seen or heard. The FART are specialists at being silent and deadly.'

Dad followed Mum. As he passed Emma, he ruffled her hair. 'And you know there's nothing worse than a silent and deadly FART,' he said.

He caught up with Mum and the two of them started talking in low voices.

'And there's nothing worse than a father who thinks he's funny,' Emma shouted after him. She tidied her hair again. 'I also don't see why we have to do the BURP's job for them. Why couldn't they send one of their own agents? I'm going to get filthy in all this dirt.'

Emma had a point, not about the dirt, but about working for the BURP. I didn't like it either. Even though I knew the Eternity Stone was too dangerous to let the FART have it, and even though I knew the BURP were doing the right thing by stealing it, I still would have felt better if the four of us had more control over what we were doing. It would have been a lot easier to work with the BURP if we'd known their whole plan and not just the bit we had to do. But I suppose we didn't have a choice. The Eternity Stone was a threat to every planet in the galaxy. We could hardly refuse to help. We were Astral Guardians. It was our job to protect planets.

It was a hot, sweaty walk to the Convention, made even

worse by the fact that Emma complained all the way – the heat was ruining her hair, she was thirsty, she was hungry and her mask was itchy. After a while I stopped listening and wished we'd left her on the X1.

Once we were at the site, I thought our appearance might cause some interest. Four people dressed as superheroes don't usually walk out of the desert. But this was a Sci-Fi Convention – the unusual was usual here. No one was bothered about us. Maybe it was because we blended in perfectly. I know I always moaned about my costume and how silly it looked, but compared to the

ones around me, mine was dull. Yellow and gold was nothing compared to the awful combinations of orange, purple, blue and green which people wore with pride. Why was it that sci-fi fans always thought aliens had no sense of colour or style? Walking among all these gaudy, garish people, I felt almost normal.

'Let's wait here for a minute,' Mum said. 'There's something I want to see.'

She stopped in front of an open-air stage which had a large crowd gathered around it.

On the stage, a group of men and women dressed all in white sat at tables signing photographs. I recognised the costumes. This was a *Galactic Warriors* exhibit. The series had been on television years ago but still had lots of devoted fans. Most of the actors were now so old it was hard to recognise them, but one in particular stood out.

His name was Gerald Talbot. He had played the main character in the series: Duke Cloudstalker. Gerald sat in the middle of the stage at a table that was slightly higher than the others. I don't think this had anything to do with Gerald thinking he was the most important. It was just that Gerald wasn't very tall. It was well known that he was sensitive about his height, his weight, and the fact that he was losing his hair.

As his fans approached, Gerald greeted them with his most famous catchphrase. 'May the power of the Source light up your life.'

'And up yours!' his fans replied.

Mum seemed to take a great interest in Gerald Talbot. I didn't know why – she never watched

the *Galactic Warriors*. I only watched it if I was bored and if I couldn't be bothered to switch over and find out if there was anything else I wanted to watch.

'Do you think he's our contact?' Emma said.

'No,' I replied. 'He's not a BURP agent. He's not even a good actor. In fact, from what I've read about him on the internet, most people think he's a bit of an old fart.'

A woman dressed in a black jacket with an official-looking badge on her arm approached Mum. She was shaped like a barrel and had muscular arms and legs. The suspicious stare she

gave the four of us made me think she was a security guard.

'Excuse me, ma'am,' the woman said, 'but can I see your tickets?'

'Of course you *can* see them,' Mum replied. 'All you have to do is use your eyes. I think what you meant to say was, *may* I see your tickets?'

The woman's mouth twisted as if she'd eaten something sour. 'All right, I get it,' she said, 'you're English. Well, don't try any of that smart talk with me. Show your tickets or get out.'

'I'm afraid we don't have any,' Mum said.

The woman didn't waste time. She pushed the four of us away from the stage and shoved us in the direction of a small hut near the entrance to the site. We didn't do anything to stop her. We couldn't. Mum had told us to act like ordinary people and not to use our powers until she said so.

Once we were inside the hut, the woman lined us up by the wall. It was a small, dusty hut where even the sunlight had a grimy glow. The woman sat on the edge of a creaking desk and held out a podgy hand. I thought she was going to ask for our tickets again. She didn't.

'All right, where's the Eternity Stone?' she said.

CHAPTER 8

So this was our contact? I have to admit, I wasn't convinced. The woman didn't look like a BURP agent. I expected someone a bit more . . . spy-looking. On the other hand, if she'd looked like a spy then she wouldn't have been a very good spy. BURP agents weren't supposed to be noticed.

'Well?' the woman said.

'You must be Clarke,' Mum replied. 'Wyndham told me you'd find us once we got here.'

The woman smiled and shook her head. 'No,

Ms Victory,' she said. 'My name's Harrison and it was Brunner who told you to wait for me at the *Galactic Warriors* exhibit. Look, I understand your caution, but if I worked for the FART, do you think Commander Dorian would have gone to all the trouble of pursuing Pohl when all she had to do was wait for him to get here and then pick him up?'

Mum said nothing.

Harrison folded her arms and stared at the floor. 'I'll be honest,' she said. 'I can't fight four Astral Guardians on my own. I couldn't even beat one of you, but if you don't give me the Eternity Stone, I will have to try to take it. The latest report I have from Brunner and his team is that they haven't been able to stop Commander Dorian launching the drones. It won't be long before they get here.'

Mum's face went pale. She took the silver cylinder from her costume and handed it to Harrison. 'Do what you have to do,' she said, 'and good luck.'

Harrison put the
cylinder inside her
jacket.

'Luck, Ms
Victory?' she
replied. 'I'm not
the one who's
going to need
luck. My ship is
ready and I'll be
off this planet in
no time at all. But

as for you ... well, you have to stay here and
protect everyone. It doesn't seem fair does it?
You've saved the galaxy and now you have to
face the FART alone. You're the ones who are
going to need the luck.' She went to the door and
opened it. 'They say you're one of the best teams
Astral Command has; well, I hope that's true. I truly
wish I could stay to help, but ...' She gave us a sad,
thoughtful smile, gazed into the sky and left,
disappearing into the crowd of sci-fi fans.

For a moment, none of us moved or spoke.

'Are we really one of the best Astral Guardian teams?' Emma said. 'I mean, I know we're a good team . . . but one of the best?' There was a cracked mirror on the wall behind the desk. Emma went to it and checked to make sure her mask was on properly. 'Is there a kind of ranking system or do people vote for us, like at an awards show or something?'

I took hold of Mum's hand and made her look at me.

'Why did Harrison say we were going to need luck?' I asked. 'On the X1, we beat Commander

Dorian's guards, and we can beat them again. What aren't you telling us?'

Mum pulled her hand away. She went to stand beside Emma and put her arms around her. They started talking together. I couldn't hear what they were saying and I was about to go after Mum when Dad's hand gripped my shoulder. He knelt down so that he could look me in the eye.

His broad shoulders blocked out the light so that his face was in shadow.

'Commander Dorian won't be sending her guards after us,' Dad said as his hand stroked my cheek. 'She won't risk her men in a straight fight. She'll send the war dogs instead.'

The war dogs? Commander Dorian didn't have any dogs. The only things she had which looked like dogs were . . .

'The metal wolves,' I said to myself. 'She's going to send the metal wolves.' I closed my eyes

and pressed my face into Dad's hand. I could feel his strength through his palm and fingers. 'But there were hundreds of them.'

'Yes, there were hundreds of them,' Dad said. 'They're attack drones and they're what Commander Dorian has sent to get the Eternity Stone back. She'll control them from the X1. She'll see and hear everything they do.'

'But there were hundreds of them,' I said again.

Dad stood up and faced Mum across the room. Emma was still looking in the mirror, only

she didn't seem to be looking at her reflection any more. She seemed to be looking at the cracks in the glass.

'But it *is* true, isn't it?' Emma said with a trembling voice. 'We *are* one of the best Astral Guardian teams?'

'Yes, sweetheart,' Mum replied. She kissed Emma's head. 'We are one of the best Astral Guardian teams.'

CHAPTER 9

We stood in the doorway of the hut, huddled together like a normal mum, dad, brother and sister, arms around each other, watching, listening and waiting. I knew we couldn't stay like this for long, but for now it was the right thing to do.

It could only have been about five minutes before we heard the first screams. The crowd started to swirl and churn like the currents of a river. Anxious faces looked around, wondering what was going on. Not even purple and green face paint could hide the fear in people's eyes. It was only when a burning car flew over our heads and crashed into an exhibition hall that the panic began. Now everyone was stumbling, tripping and falling over each other in their rush to get away. It was a terrified scramble as stalls toppled over, marquees ripped, flag poles cracked and banners were trampled underfoot.

I saw the first metal wolf on the far side of the site. It marched towards us, striding over cars as if

they were stepping-stones. It was soon joined by a second, then a third and a fourth. I stopped counting by the time I got to eight. I only had to watch the wolves to realise the numbers didn't matter. Nothing stood in their way. If a wolf couldn't crush something under its metal feet, then a white bolt of energy flashed from its snout and blew the obstacle away.

Camper vans and pick-up trucks turned into balls of fire.

A surge of terrified people thudded into the hut and threatened to knock it over. We lost our balance and fell back as the door slammed in our faces, forced shut by the

weight of bodies outside. The walls shook, the floor shuddered, the joints that held the hut together creaked and groaned. We found ourselves sliding backwards. The hut was turning over on its side! The desk slammed into the wall and the cracked mirror broke.

'Hang on, everyone!' Dad shouted.

He flew up to the ceiling and put his shoulders against the metal. The hut began to rise. Dad held out his hands.

'Louise, Emma, grab hold of me. Mark, get in the air and keep your weight off the walls and floor. This thing could break apart at any minute!'

We did as we were told. As the hut rose from the ground, the door fell open.

I wished the door hadn't fallen open. Dad may have been able to see where he was going, but the wolves could see us. Tin huts don't usually fly by themselves – even at a Sci-Fi Convention. A line of glittering snouts took aim.

'Going up!' Dad cried.

And up we went. Bolts of energy exploded

under us. One caught the side of the hut. A metal panel flew off and went whirling to the ground. This was too much for the rusted screws and joints that held everything together. There was a crack and a snap. The floor, ceiling and walls fell away.

'I've got this!' Emma cried. She used the power of her mind to catch each of the falling pieces and threw them at the wolves. The desk shattered against one without leaving a mark. The metal panels did a bit more damage. The roof sliced into the neck of a wolf and cut the head off so that it hung loose on a tangle of wires and cables. The wolf kept moving, except it stumbled

around blindly until it crossed the path of another wolf and was blown to pieces.

'Robert!' Mum shouted. 'They're only interested in us. Fly into the desert so that we can fight them without anyone getting hurt!'

Only it was too late to stop anyone getting hurt.

As Dad turned in the direction of the desert, I saw two terrified children below me, clinging together as people ran past. Where were their parents? A wolf was marching towards them. The children were going to be crushed under its feet!

An elderly man, dressed all in white, dashed

through the crowd, climbed onto an overturned packing crate and threw himself onto the back of the wolf. He had a long, metal pipe in his hand. It looked like a piece of scaffolding. He smashed the pipe down on the wolf's head, hitting its eyes. He managed to break one, but the wolf didn't change direction. It still headed for the children.

I flew down, thinking I'd get the children out of the way and then help the man. But before I could do anything, someone in the crowd scooped up the children and carried them off. That only left the man. I darted towards him, but in the few seconds it had taken me to change course, the wolf had thrown the man off and stamped on him.

The man lay motionless in the sand. As I landed beside his mangled body, I recognised his face. It was the actor, Gerald Talbot. There was nothing I could do for him. He may have played a hero on television but he'd also had the courage to be a hero for real – a courage that had cost him his life.

The wolf that had killed Gerald turned towards me. Sunlight flashed from its one good eye.

'If you want a fight,' I said, 'come and get it.'

I was already in the air as a bolt of energy flashed under my feet. It hit another wolf and blew the mechanical monster apart.

I followed Dad, Mum and Emma as they sped away from the site. It was like flying through a fireworks display. Energy crackled and flashed all around us. Dad soon found a place to land. It was far enough away from the site to be out of range of the wolves but, as soon as I landed, I heard their metal feet stomp across the desert.

Mum snapped out our orders. 'Robert, you have to smash as many of the drones as possible. Emma, slow them down so that your father only fights one at a time. Mark, you and I will have to use flight and speed to get them to shoot each other.' She looked at Emma and me. 'And don't try to use illusions or invisibility. These machines will have all sorts of sensors. They won't be fooled by what they see or don't see.'

Mum fell silent.

The  and

of the wolves got louder.

'I know it's not much of a plan,' she said, 'but if we don't make a stand here, Commander Dorian will attack the city in order to make us fight. The FART will do everything they can to get the Eternity Stone back and once they find out we've handed it to the BURP, we'll be of no use to them. They'll make our deaths as painful as possible.'

Dad held Mum's hand and kissed her. 'It's a good plan, Louise,' he said. 'It'll work.'

'Of course it will,' I said. 'We've been in worse situations before.'

Actually, I couldn't think of a time when we'd been in a worse situation, but no one needed to hear that. What we needed was the bravery to fight a battle we knew we were going to lose – the kind of bravery Gerald Talbot had shown.

Emma stared across the desert at the line of glistening metal. 'And,' she said, putting her hands on her hips the way Dad did before a fight, 'we're one of the best teams Astral Command has. I don't think the FART realise just who they're dealing with.'

And that was it – there was no more time for words. It was time for action.

Dad led the way. He flew at the nearest wolf, dodged an energy bolt, swung round and ripped the wolf's head off with one hand. He then

dived at a second and punched through its side. Flying from wolf to wolf, he littered the desert with heads and legs, leaving behind a trail of burning carcasses.

Emma did a great job of making sure Dad only had one wolf to fight at a time. Spinning,

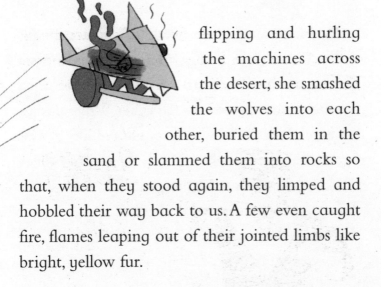

flipping and hurling the machines across the desert, she smashed the wolves into each other, buried them in the sand or slammed them into rocks so that, when they stood again, they limped and hobbled their way back to us. A few even caught fire, flames leaping out of their jointed limbs like bright, yellow fur.

As for me and Mum, we didn't do too badly either. We sped around in circles – me in the air and Mum on the ground – forcing the wolves to fire their energy bolts at each other. White flashes left black holes from which oil poured like blood. Soon, the desert looked like a scrapyard full of smoking metal and burning oil. The air was so thick with smoke, it was difficult to see.

Maybe that's why our luck ran out.

It was Mum who got hit first. I don't know how. I saw her limp towards Dad and fall before she could reach him. There was a wolf close behind her. Dad

flew straight at the wolf and smashed it to pieces, but the wolf managed to fire an energy bolt just as Dad struck. The bolt didn't hit Dad directly, but the blast sent him hurtling backwards. He landed badly and thudded into a rock. He rolled onto his hands and knees, crawled towards Mum and collapsed. Mum managed to drag herself to him, but then she slumped across his unconscious body.

'Mark!' Emma shouted. 'What do we do now?'

I didn't have a clue. My only thought was to get Mum and Dad as far away from here as possible. I flew down to them, thinking that somehow Emma and I could get them out of the desert using our combined powers. But there were too many wolves and we were surrounded.

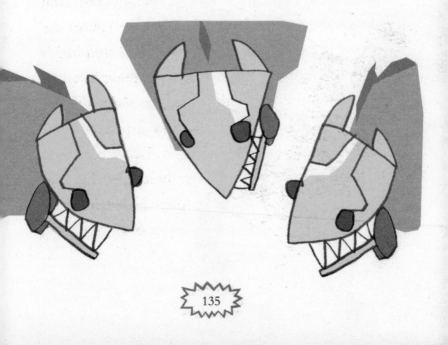

Emma ran to my side and we both crouched over Mum and Dad, trying to shield them with our bodies – not that it would make a difference. Nothing could stop the wolves now.

A circle of shining, metal heads bore down on us.

Only they didn't attack. Instead, they remained motionless, the low hum of their motors the only sound in the desert – apart from our rasping breaths and the whine of a spaceship's engines.

It flew out of the sun and hovered over the wolves, its exhausts blowing up huge, swirling clouds of dirt as its knife-shaped shadow cut across the sand. Long and angular, with more sharp edges than curves, the ship landed and its engines shut down with a hiss.

Even before the hiss had faded, Commander Dorian had thrown open a hatch and was striding across the desert towards us.

CHAPTER 10

I suppose I should have expected Commander Dorian to be there at the end. She wasn't the kind of person to send someone else to gloat. No, she'd make sure that the last thing we saw was the triumphant leer on her face.

A small group of guards filed out of the shuttle and ran to catch up with her. They took up position close to the wolves as Commander Dorian's shadow fell across us. She stood with her arms folded, staring at the ground. Sand crunched under her boots.

'My offer is simple,' she said, her voice toneless and almost too quiet to hear. 'Give me the Eternity Stone and I will order my guards to shoot you. Make me ask for the Stone a second time and I will order my war dogs to tear you apart. Either way, you die and I get the Stone. The only mercy I will show you is the choice of dying slowly or quickly.'

Mum groaned and pulled herself up so that she lay against Dad. I couldn't see any blood, but she nursed her right leg and winced whenever it moved. Dad was still unconscious. His costume was torn across the chest and there were bloodstains on his mask.

Emma looked at Mum and Dad and clenched her fists. Like me, she wanted to do something, but what could we do? There were only two of us against the guards and the wolves. We couldn't fight Commander Dorian and defend Mum and Dad at the same time.

'Wait, Dorian!' Mum raised her hand. 'It would

be a mistake to kill us. We don't
have the Eternity Stone. We've . . .
I've hidden it. If you kill us,
you'll never find it again.'

'Really, Ms Victory?' Commander
Dorian looked round at the desert.
'And where have you hidden it? Out there in the
sand? Of course you have. After all, what would
an Astral Guardian do with the most powerful
weapon in the galaxy except bury it? No, Ms
Victory, you still have the Eternity Stone.' Dorian
bent down and grabbed Mum's injured leg.
'Because if you don't have it, that can only mean

you have passed it on to Pohl's contact and, if that's the case, then I'll have you and your team taken to the X1 where you will be used to test some very painful interrogation techniques. One way or another, I'll get the Stone back. You'll either tell me where it is or I'll tear this planet apart looking for it. The X1 is scanning for any ship that tries to leave Earth's orbit. We are monitoring all communications for any information that may lead us to it. I have more attack drones ready to launch against any country or city where the Stone may be located.'

Mum tried not to cry out as Dorian's fingers dug into her skin.

'No matter what I have to do, Ms Victory, I will find the Stone! However, in case you doubt my determination, perhaps a brief demonstration will convince you that I mean what I say. Choose which one of your team will die. Is it to be Captain Valiant, Moon Girl or . . .' Commander Dorian frowned at me. 'What was your name again?'

Terrific. I was about to be shot or torn apart by mechanical wolves, and she couldn't even remember my name. If anyone ever got round to writing the story of my life, they might as well leave a  blank on the title page and let people write in whatever name they wanted.

'Dynamic Boy,' I said.

'Oh, yes, Dynamic Boy.' Commander Dorian moved to stand beside the wolves. 'Well, Ms Victory, have you made a choice?'

Mum went to speak but the only sound she made was a gasp of pain. At the same time, Dad groaned and opened his eyes. He also tried to sit up but fell flat on his back again. He blinked at the sky and turned his head to look at the wolves. He squinted and grinned.

'If you want my advice, Dorian,' he said, 'you'll surrender now. Raise your hands and you might save yourself. As for your men, I think they're finished.'

Commander Dorian ignored him. She pointed at me. 'Kill him,' she said.

A wolf jerked towards me, its metal jaws snapping open. I scrambled back, knowing that my only chance was to fly off. But I also knew that as

soon as I left the ground one of the guards would shoot me down. Even Emma couldn't help. If she did, there was a good chance she'd also be shot.

The wolf's jaws slashed at the air, its legs kicked up the sand and its head blocked out the sun. I heard motors whine and joints clang. I saw the metal teeth lunge towards me and then . . . nothing. The teeth were gone, the head was gone and the wolf was gone. One moment it was there, about to rip me to pieces, and then it wasn't. All that remained of the metal monster was a spiral of blue light.

'Good shot,' Dad said.

Another wolf vanished in exactly the same way, then another, and another. Faster than my eye could follow them, the wolves turned into spirals of blue light. The machines were disappearing in groups of two, three and four, leaving behind only footprints in the sand.

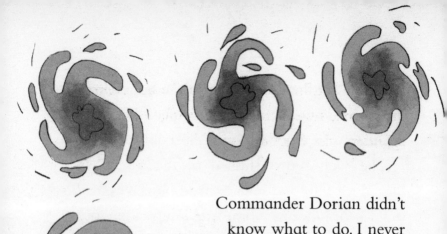

Commander Dorian didn't know what to do. I never thought I'd see her look confused, but she watched in amazement as the wolves vanished. Realising she had to do something, she turned to her guards, but they were disappearing as well. In the time it took her to bark an order, there was no one left to obey it. Even her spaceship had gone, the desert glittering with dozens of blue spirals, which faded away like guttering candles — until Commander Dorian stood alone with four Astral Guardians and a BURP agent.

It was Harrison, the security guard at the Convention. She strolled towards us, whistling to herself and holding what seemed to be a sort of rifle. It had a long, black barrel. In the centre of the barrel, slotted into the metal, was a silver cylinder – the Eternity Stone.

Harrison approached Commander Dorian and raised the rifle. For a moment, the two women stared at each other. Both smiled, but it was for different reasons. I saw determination on Harrison's face and defiance on Commander Dorian's. As Harrison fired, her smile turned into a weary frown. As Commander Dorian disappeared in a spiral of blue light, her smile became a malicious laugh which faded as quickly as the light.

Harrison rested the rifle on her shoulder. She looked at us and shrugged.

'Well, I couldn't really leave you to fight this battle on your own, could I?' she said. 'After all, you helped save the galaxy. It would have been a bit ungrateful for me to walk away and do nothing. Besides, once I got back to my ship, I thought it would be a good idea to make sure the Eternity Stone worked properly. We'd already stolen enough technical data to know *how* it works, but without the Stone itself, we couldn't be sure it *would* work.' She patted the rifle. 'Now we know it does.'

Dad tried to get up again. He was still a bit groggy and I didn't think his legs would hold his weight. They did, just about. Unfortunately, as he got up, Mum slid off him and hit the ground hard. She screamed in pain and Dad said sorry lots of times as Emma took hold of Mum with her thoughts and raised her gently off the ground.

'My ship's not far from here,' Harrison said. 'You look like you could do with a lift. I don't think it would be a good idea to stay around here much

longer. After what happened at the Convention, there are a lot of people in uniforms running around. Now, unless you want to answer some very awkward questions, I suggest you come with me.'

'I have one awkward question,' Mum said.

Harrison kicked at the sand and chuckled to herself.

'Yes, Ms Victory, I'm sure you do. But you know I'm not going to answer it. I'm a BURP agent.

My job is to keep secrets. If you want to know what's going to happen to the Eternity Stone, I'm not going to tell you. All I will say is that you don't have to worry about the Stone, the FART or the X1 any more. Now we have what we want, and Commander Dorian is out of the way, we can deal with the FART on our own. You've done your job and we're very grateful for your help.'

Harrison turned and set off across the desert, whistling again.

The four of us watched her. There was something about the way she walked and the way she whistled which made me very angry. After everything we'd been through, after everything we'd done for the BURP, surely they couldn't just take the Eternity Stone and walk away?

'OK, everyone,' Mum said, 'let's go. Harrison's right. We can't stay here. We need to get back home so that I can contact Astral Command. They can deal with this now. I've had enough of all this spy stuff.'

And so had I. Mum couldn't walk, Dad was dazed and groggy, Emma looked like she was going to cry, and I was exhausted. Even a slow walk across the desert seemed like hard work. To make matters worse, Emma ran across and gave me a hug! I could hardly breathe. When she let go, there were tears on her cheeks.

'I thought . . .' she said, '. . . when that metal thing attacked you . . . I thought . . . Well, you know . . .'

She sniffed and thumped me. 'Don't do anything as stupid as that again!'

Yes, I'd definitely had enough of spy stuff if it meant my sister started giving me hugs.

Emma strode off to join Mum and Dad. Her thoughts still held Mum off the ground as the three of them followed Harrison. Glancing over

her shoulder, she shouted, 'Come on, we're not waiting for you.'

But they didn't have to wait. I wanted to go home as much as they did. I ran after them and, together, me, my mum, my dad and my sister walked into the . . . well, it wasn't exactly the sunset. It was only mid-afternoon. And we didn't really walk – Mum hovered, Dad limped, Emma trudged and I plodded.

But at least we were going home.

HAVE YOU READ...

REVENGE OF THE BLACK PHANTOM

Mark Taylor seems to be an average schoolboy, but he's really Dynamic Boy!
He and his family – Captain Valiant, Ms Victory and Moon Girl – are a superhero team. If only his name, costume and superpower weren't so rubbish, Dynamic Boy might enjoy saving the world from baddies . . .
But when people start turning into monsters, they all realise this is no ordinary baddy – it's the revenge of the Black Phantom.

RETURN OF
THE SILVER CYBORG

Mark Taylor, aka Dynamic Boy, and his
superhero family are under threat from an evil
techno-genius. The Silver Cyborg's got a devious
new plan – he's going to trap them in
the world of Dynamic Boy's mind!

How will their superpowers
save them from the dangers
of Mark's imagination?
And will Mark ever
survive the
embarrassment of his
family seeing his
deepest, secret wishes?
It could be his biggest
challenge ever!

CAPTAIN VALIANT

And me

THE LAIR OF DR MACDETH

On a weekend break to Scotland, our favourite
superhero family get captured and taken to a
remote castle owned by a creepy scientist.
Dr MacDeth needs a few extra body parts —
and who better to provide them than his new
prisoners? And that's if they survive the
terrifying results of his previous experiments,
all hungry for fresh meat!

piccadillypress.co.uk/children

Go online to discover:

☆ more authors you'll love

☆ competitions

☆ sneak peeks inside books

☆ fun activities and downloads